Cub Shrugs

Time to Read® is an early reader program designed to guide children to literacy success regardless of age or grade level. The program's three levels correspond to stages of reading readiness, making book selection straightforward, and assuring that when it's time for a child to read, the right book is waiting.

— Level — **1**

Beginning to Read

- Large, simple type
- Basic vocabulary
- Word repetition
- Strong illustration support

— Level — **2**

Reading with Help

- Short sentences
- Engaging stories
- Simple dialogue
- Illustration support

— Level — **3**

Reading Independently

- Longer sentences
- Harder words
- Short paragraphs
- Increased story complexity

For Michael, my sweet cub—LHH

To all the wonderful staff at Favours Day
Nursery, Moulton. Thank you.—AW

Library of Congress Cataloging-in-Publication data
is on file with the publisher.

Text copyright © 2020 by Lori Haskins Houran
Illustrations copyright © 2020 by Albert Whitman & Company
Illustrations by Alex Willmore
First published in the United States of America
in 2020 by Albert Whitman & Company
ISBN 978-0-8075-7197-2 (hardcover)
ISBN 978-0-8075-7195-8 (ebook)

Printed in China
10 9 8 7 6 5 4 3 2 1 RRD 24 23 22 21 20

Designed by Valerie Hernández

TIME TO READ® is a registered trademark
of Albert Whitman & Company.

For more information about Albert Whitman & Company,
visit our website at www.albertwhitman.com.

Animal
Time

Cub Shrugs

Lori Haskins Houran

illustrated by
Alex Willmore

Albert Whitman & Company
Chicago, Illinois

Cub is glum.

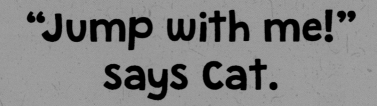

"Jump with me!" says Cat.

Cub shrugs.

"Kick with me!"
says Ape.

Cub shrugs.

Cub shrugs.

"Bend with me!"
says Sloth.

Cub shrugs.

"Hmmm,"
says Sloth.

"Say that again,"
says Bird.

"Hmmm?"
says Sloth.

Bird makes a plan.

Bird makes a band!

Sloth hums.
Cat strums.
Ape drums.

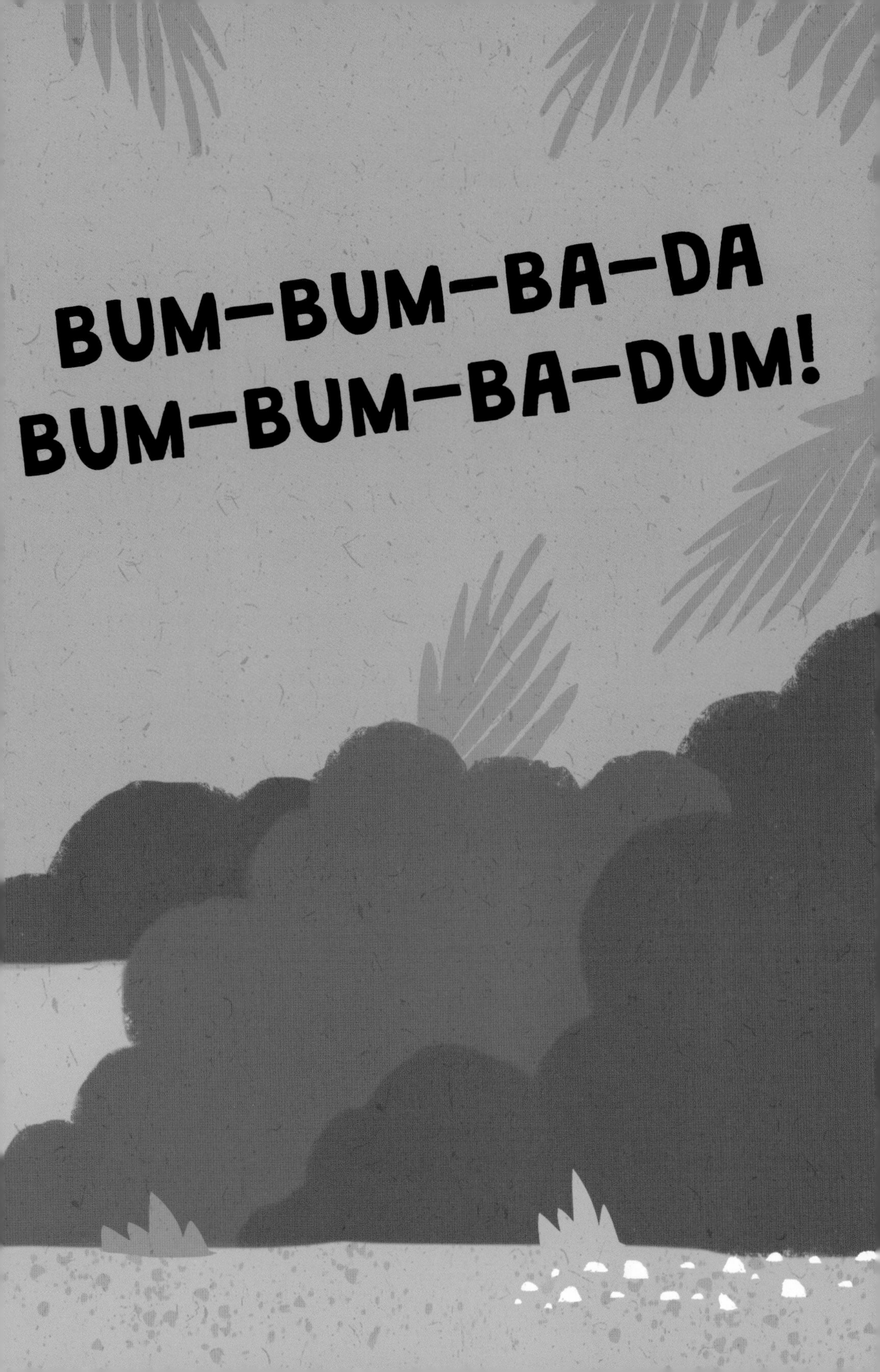
BUM-BUM-BA-DA
BUM-BUM-BA-DUM!

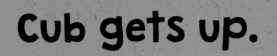

Cub gets up.

Cub gets DOWN!

He jumps!

He kicks!

He spins!

He bends!

He moves until the music ends.

Cub hugs.